Community Learning & Libraries
Cymuned Ddysgu a Llyfrgelloedd

This item should be returned or renewed by the
last date stamped below.

Newport
CITY COUNCIL
CYNGOR DINAS
Casnewydd

To renew visit:

www.newport.gov.uk/libraries

For
TOM *"Why do they have trees?"* BENJAMIN,
CLARE, SARAH, CONNIE, MATILDA & MILES

Other books
by Raymond Briggs

THE SNOWMAN
FATHER CHRISTMAS
FATHER CHRISTMAS GOES ON HOLIDAY
JIM AND THE BEANSTALK
FUNGUS THE BOGEYMAN
THE BEAR

PUFFIN BOOKS

UK | USA | Canada | Ireland | Australia | India | New Zealand | South Africa

Puffin Books is part of the Penguin Random House group of companies
whose addresses can be found at global.penguinrandomhouse.com.
www.penguin.co.uk   www.puffin.co.uk   www.ladybird.co.uk

 Penguin
Random House
UK

First published by Jonathan Cape 2001
First Published by Red Fox 2002
Published by Puffin Books 2016
005

Copyright © Raymond Briggs, 2001
The moral right of the author/illustrator has been asserted

Printed in China
A CIP catalogue record for this book is available from the British Library

ISBN: 978–0–141–37405–5

All correspondence to:
Puffin Books, Penguin Random House Children's
80 Strand, London WC2R 0RL

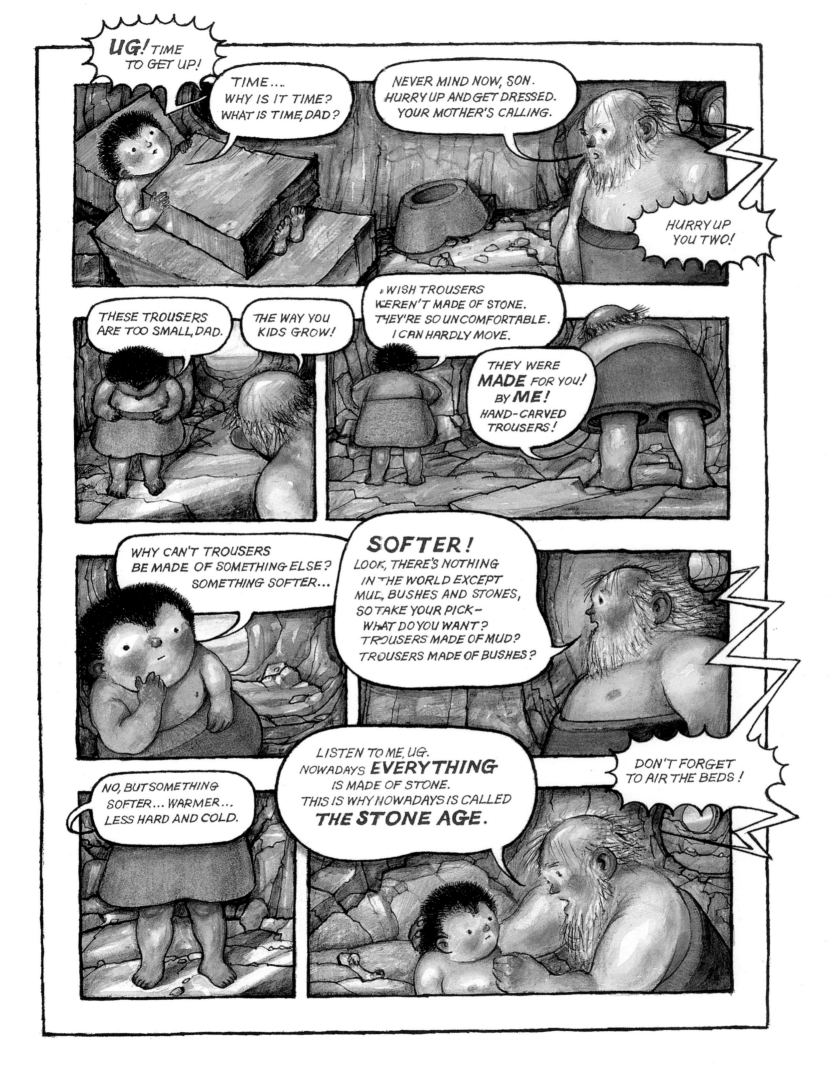

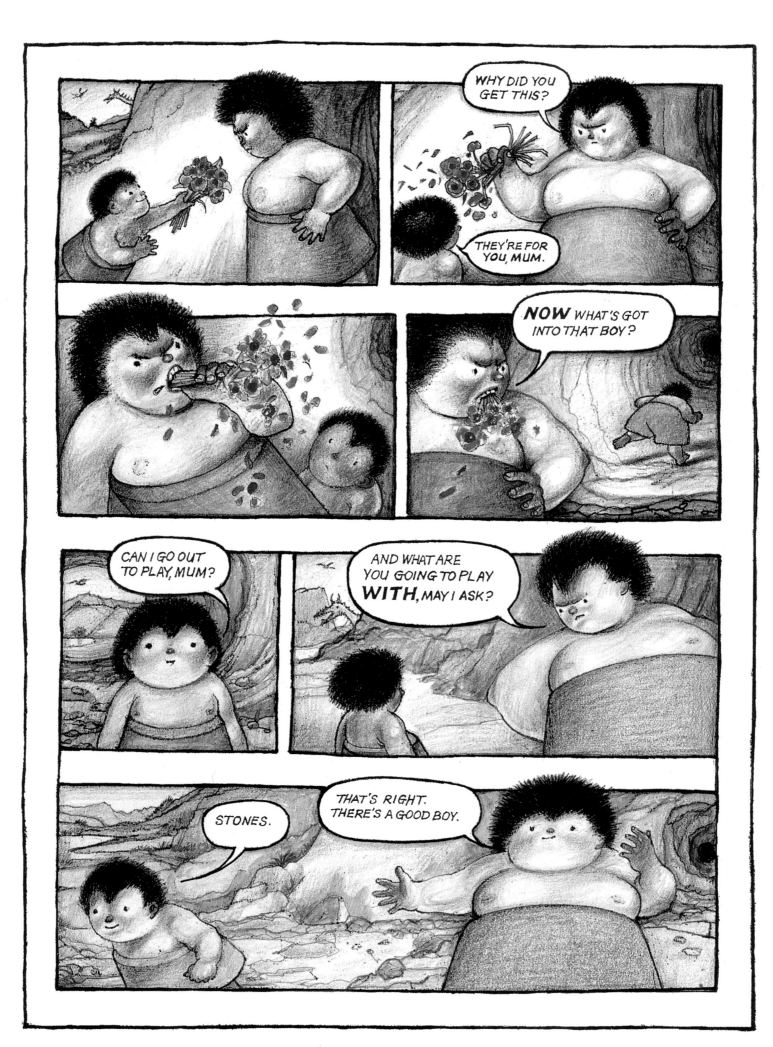

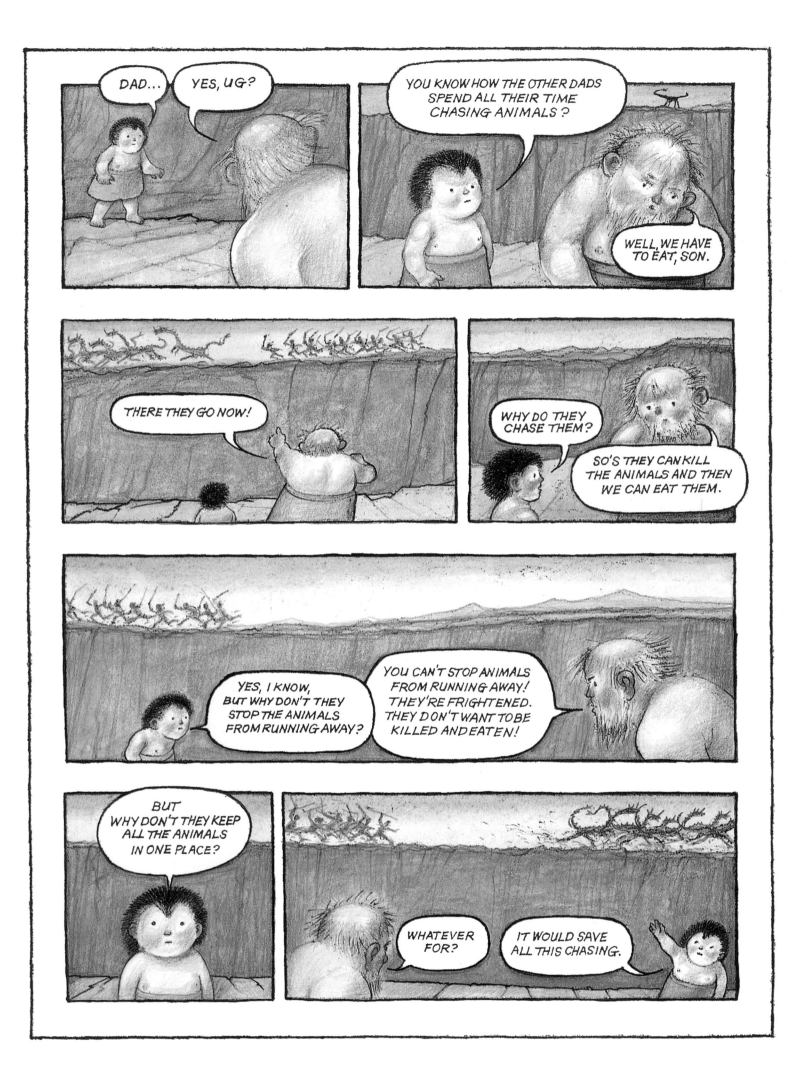

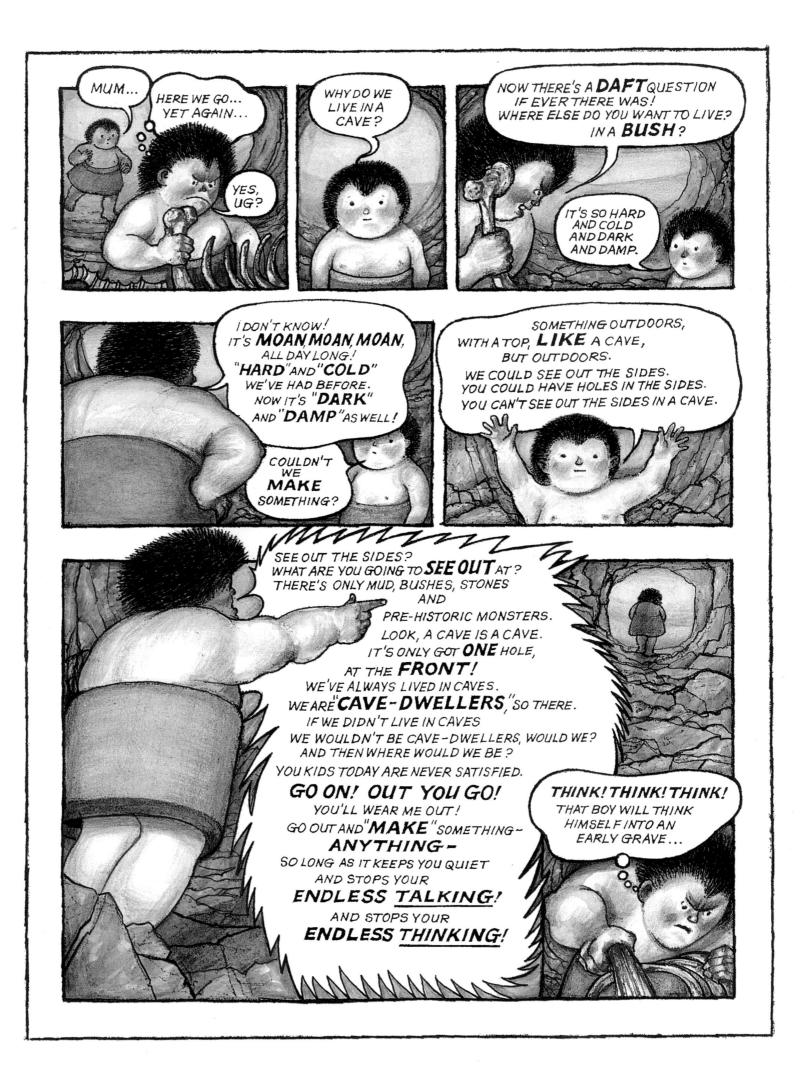

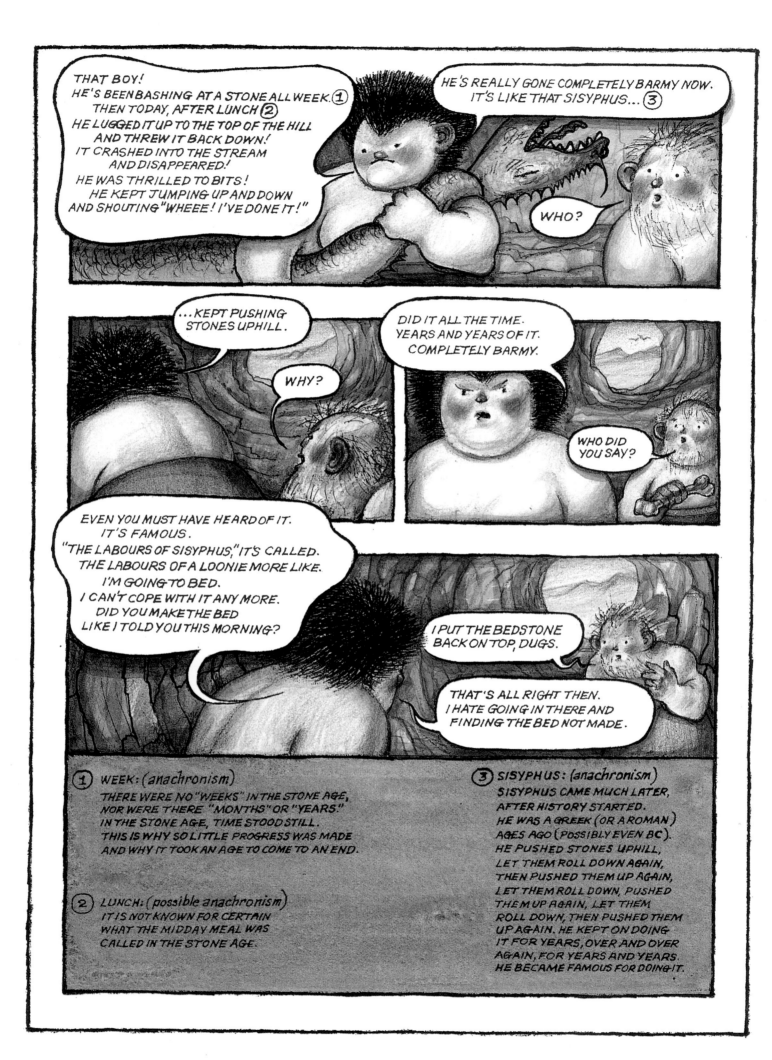

② SUMMER HOLIDAY: (anachronism)
SUMMER HOLIDAYS WERE UNKNOWN
IN THE STONE AGE.
ALTHOUGH NO ONE WENT TO WORK,
THE STRUGGLE FOR SURVIVAL WAS SO HARD,
DUE TO THE STONY CONDITIONS, THE MUD
AND THE ENORMOUS NUMBER OF BUSHES
THAT THERE WAS LITTLE TIME LEFT
FOR HOLIDAYS. SO THEY WERE UNKNOWN.
    FURTHERMORE, THE CLIMATE WAS
COMPLETELY DIFFERENT TO THE PRESENT
DAY AND "SUMMER" WAS PROBABLY
UNKNOWN DUE TO THE CLIMATE
BEING COMPLETELY DIFFERENT.

③ BOOTS: (anachronism)
BOOTS WERE ALMOST UNKNOWN IN THE
STONE AGE. ANIMALS WITH LEATHERY
SKINS HAD NOT YET EVOLVED, AS ALL
THE ANIMALS WERE STILL PRE-HISTORIC
MONSTERS. SUCH BOOTS AS DID EXIST
WERE MADE OF STONE AND WERE
ALMOST AS UNCOMFORTABLE AS THE
STONE TROUSERS. SO THEY WERE NEVER
USED. CONSEQUENTLY, NO STONE AGE
BOOT HAS EVER BEEN FOUND, AND
OF COURSE, NEVER A PAIR.